Tales from the
The Courageous Ant

MW00764175

Tales from the Shell:
The Courageous Ant

Written by
Valentina Arango

Illustrated by
Matthew Holland

El Pozo
October 2012

© valentina arango
© illustrations, matthew holland
© ediciones el pozo

First edition. October 2012

Isbn 978-0-9821364-7-8

Once upon a
time there
was a little but
very strong ant.

Unfortunately this ant's entire family was sick.
His mission was to take care of them
and make sure they were safe.

One day a storm was going to blow in.
The strong little ant dug and dug to make shelter
for his family.

He was almost finished digging when suddenly
the storm came.

The strong little ant, then, put as much of his family
in the burrow as possible.

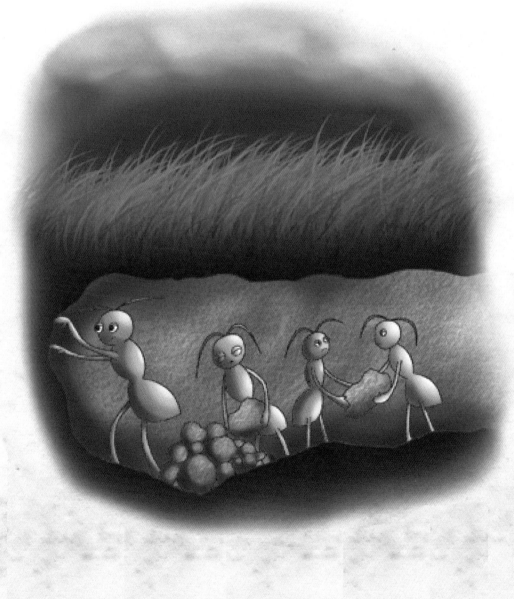

In the end the little ant and his sick brother were
left out of the burrow.
The strong ant then took his brother's hand and led
him through the storm.
Together they looked for a safe place to stay.

Finally, in all the
chaos, they saw an abandoned turtle shell.

Mr, Emis Turtle, the turtle that used to live in the shell,
was tired of being normal.
He was tired of the boring life that he was living.

One day Emis decided to leave his shell behind
and start a new and adventurous life.

The little ant and his brother entered the shell
and looked around.
The walls of the shell were covered in pictures.
What did the pictures mean?

Did they mean that the turtle who lived there
would be the one to help them?

This turtle was going to be the friend they needed.
This turtle was divine.

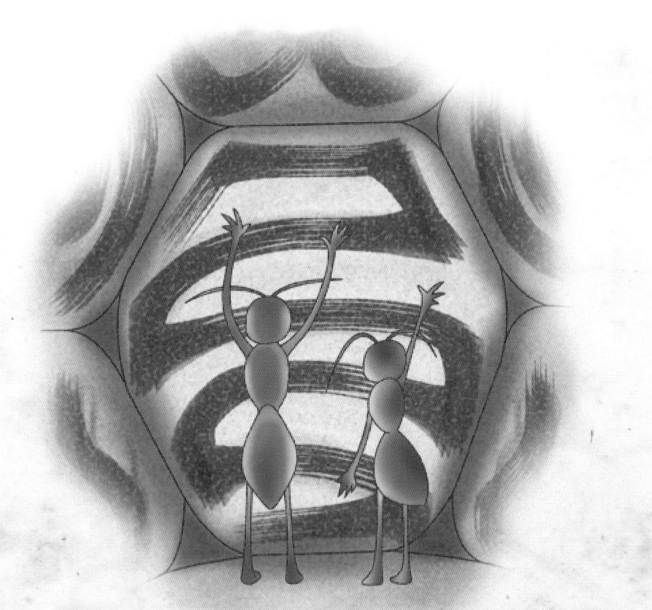

At that moment the strong ant and his little brother
decided to go on a mission to find the turtle,
follow him
and protect him.

After the storm, all the ants met up,
and the strong little ant
told them of their find.

He then brought all the ants to the shell, to show
them why they must begin their mission.
When the ants saw the engravings
they did not doubt for an instant
that this turtle was
The Divine Turtle.

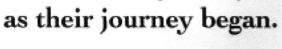

The ants gathered their belongings and
prepared themselves for the quest.
The ants sang loudly and joyously
as their journey began.

As they walked on, days passed. The ants still had not reached the turtle, and the sick ants started passing away.

The once large and joyous group was now sad and hopeless.

The strong little ant, however, still had hope.
He continued the journey strongly and proudly.

More days passed, the large group was down
to a journey of few.

The more the time passed the less ants
there were.

Soon only the strong ant and his brother were left.

At this point the strong ant was almost
regretting
and doubting the mission.

The two ants continued quietly and with very little hope.

After one week of journey the strong ant's little brother passed away.

The strong little ant was devastated and ready to give up.

The strong little ant sat on a pebble, and cried.

After several hours of crying he made up his mind.

He decided he was going to walk for only one more day.

If by sunset he had not found the turtle,
he would give up.

That night the little ant rested.

The next morning he continued his journey,
he walked and walked.

Soon it was sunset.
The poor little ant fell on his knees crying.

The journey was over.

The next morning
the strong little ant woke up
to loud and thundering footsteps.

Frightened,
he opened his eyes slowly
and what he saw!

Several steps away from him was

The Shell-lessTurtle.

The strong little ant's eyes lit up and he ran to the turtle. He bowed at Emis's feet and screamed.

"Oh almighty and all powerful turtle! I am here as your follower, please accept my humility!"

Emis looked down at the ant, confused for a moment,
and then with a smile said,

"I *was* a little hungry."

NOM NOM NOM

Mr.Emis Turtle ate the strong little ant in three savory chews.

He leaned back on a tree and took his nap.

THE
END

15274124R00022

Made in the USA
Charleston, SC
26 October 2012